# THE GHASTLY McNASTYS

Lyn ~~Gardner~~ ardian and goes to the theatre five or six times a week, which should leave no time for writing books ... But actually she has written several children's books, including the very successful *Olivia* series. She lives by Richmond Park.

Ros Asquith is a cartoonist for *The Guardian*, and has written and illustrated many books. *Letters from an Alien Schoolboy* was shortlisted for the Roald Dahl Funny Prize, and *The Great Big Book of Families*, which she illustrated, won the SLA Information Book Award. She lives in North London.

# THE GHASTLY McNASTYS

## RAIDERS OF THE LOST SHARK

# LYN GARDNER & ROS ASQUITH

*Piccadilly*

*For Hannah L — L.G.*

*To Lola, Lenny and Lucille — R.A.*

First published in Great Britain in 2014
by Piccadilly Press
A Templar/Bonnier publishing company
Deepdene Lodge, Deepdene Avenue, Dorking, Surrey, RH5 4AT
www.piccadillypress.co.uk

A catalogue record for this book is available
from the British Library

ISBN: 978 1 84812 363 2 (paperback)

1 3 5 7 9 10 8 6 4 2

Printed in the UK by CPI Group (UK) Ltd, Croydon, CR0 4YY
Cover design by Simon Davis
Cover illustration by Ros Asquith

# WARNING!

Do not leave
this book unattended
at any time.

The McNastys may try
to escape from the pages,
and if they do things
could turn
VERY NASTY
indeed.

# RAIDERS OF THE LOST SHARK

OPEN AUDITIONS
at
LITTLE SNORING CASTLE

Dress code: PIRATE

# Chapter 1

The whale gave an enormous burp. She had been feeling queasy for some weeks, as if she had swallowed something bad. And she had. She had swallowed the McNasty twins, who were the nastiest

Poor Mrs Slime, who was the McNastys' second mate, used to sew these patches on.

pirates ever to sail the Seven Seas. The McNastys were Gruesome and Grisly. And that was just their names. They were also greedy and grouchy and grumbly and very, very grubby. They never changed their underwear and they almost never brushed their teeth. If they did, they sometimes tried to use the same brush that they used to brush their hair. The brush was covered in grease and grime and tasted of earwig droppings. The McNastys hated brushing their teeth. They also hated all children, and they hated two children in particular: Tat and Hetty, who had stopped them from finding the lost treasure of Little Snoring.

It was because of Tat and Hetty's courage and resourcefulness that the Ghastly McNastys were stuck inside the belly of the whale with no way of getting out. They had tried tunnelling out using their hairbrush, but without success because

whale blubber is very thick.

It was stinky and slimy inside the whale. In fact it was so slimy that the McNastys kept falling over on their bottoms, which made them more bad-tempered than ever. They took all their bad temper out on

SQUEAKY PANTS

Captain Grisly's teddy bear and their parrot, Pegleg Polly.

The whale gave another ginormous

# BUUUUUUURRP.

It was so loud that many thousands of miles away icebergs wobbled and penguins lost their footing and fell off them, and they had to find some very tall ladders to climb back up.

**BUURRP**

The whale burped again.

'Sweaty socks,' shrieked Captain Gruesome as he slithered along the entire length of the whale's enormous tummy.

'Squeaky pants,' yelled Captain Grisly as he was swamped in a tidal wave of the whale's digestive juices. He grabbed his teddy for comfort.

There was a terrible sound as the whale gave a gigantic belch and the McNasty twins found themselves hurtling up the whale's throat, past her teeth and out through her mouth in a massive plume of hot breath and sea water. They were followed by Pegleg Polly, the parrot (who disliked the McNastys as much as anyone and everyone).

Such was the force generated by the whale's burp that the McNastys sailed

through the air for miles and miles, eventually landing with a terrible thump on a beach with dazzling white sand. A flock of passing seagulls took the opportunity to plop all over the McNastys – something they had been dying to do for years but hadn't dared before.

'Ugh,' shrieked Captain Gruesome.

'Ouch,' yelled Captain Grisly.

The McNastys lifted their heads and looked warily around, checking for children and spiders. They loathed them both.

'Where are we?' asked Gruesome. His head felt as if an elephant had done a tap dance on it.

Captain Grisly saw the white sands, the rolling green hills, the lighthouse and the

# BIG, SCARY, VERY **DARK**, DENSE FOREST

## WHERE NO ONE IN THEIR RIGHT MIND WOULD WANT TO GO.

'We are exactly where we want to be,' he said with a wicked grin.

'At the Captain Syd Memorial Bank on the day they are handing out free money, gold bars and unlimited ice cream?' asked Captain Gruesome hopefully.

Captain Grisly shook his head. 'We're back where we began, in Little Snoring.'

Captain Gruesome looked scared. 'I don't want to meet those horrible children again or that exceptionally nasty cat called Dog,' he whimpered. 'And I don't want to walk through the

**WHERE NO ONE IN THEIR RIGHT MIND WOULD WANT TO GO**

because it was horrid. And there were spiders. I don't want to end up inside a whale again either. It is not a sensible way to travel.' He sighed. Captain Gruesome hadn't felt so miserable since the day his brother had

given him a bag of what
he had told him were
chocolate raisins and later
confessed were rabbit
droppings – but only after
Gruesome had gobbled
them all up.

Captain Grisly glared at his brother who
he thought was being a great big wimpy
cupcake. 'Are you a pirate or a great big
wimpy cupcake?' he demanded.

Cupcake

Pirate

Captain Gruesome looked down at himself. 'I'm a pirate, you bumbling idiot,' he screeched. 'And no self-respecting pirate would pass up an opportunity to get his hands on

CAPTAIN SYD'S LOST TREASURE,'

His piggy little eyes gleamed. 'Where is it?' he said, looking hungrily around.

Captain Grisly pointed up the beach to a small shop. Outside there was a sign

advertising the latest edition of the *Little Snoring Gazette*. It read:

'Sweaty socks! Let's go and find it immediately before those vile, villainous, treasure-snatching children and that cat called Dog get there and snaffle all the emeralds and ingots and pearls,' said Captain Gruesome, greed overcoming his fear.

'Squeaky pants! Let's hurry,' said Captain Grisly. 'When we've found the treasure we'll take our revenge on those horrific children and that cat called Dog and feed them to the sharks.'

# Chapter 2

(The plot thickens. I normally find that gravy granules or a little glue on the end of my quill pen does the job quite nicely.)

Trevor Augustus Trout, known to everyone as Tat, and his best friend, Hetty, were sitting side by side in class trying to solve some hideously horrible maths problems set by their teacher, Miss Green.

They were the kind of maths problems that make you feel as if your brain has turned into squirming worms, which are being gobbled alive by hungry ostriches. Unless you are Hetty, who was the cleverest girl in Little Snoring and possibly the cleverest brainiac in the entire universe. Her brain loved maths problems – the more hideous and horrible the better. Everyone always said that Hetty knew everything (which wasn't quite true because she definitely didn't know where Captain Syd's treasure was buried in Little Snoring).

It was the last day of the school year and to Miss Green's disgust many of the children had arrived late. This was because of a massive traffic jam caused by lorries heading to Little Snoring Castle where the big Hollywood movie, *Raiders of the Lost Shark*,

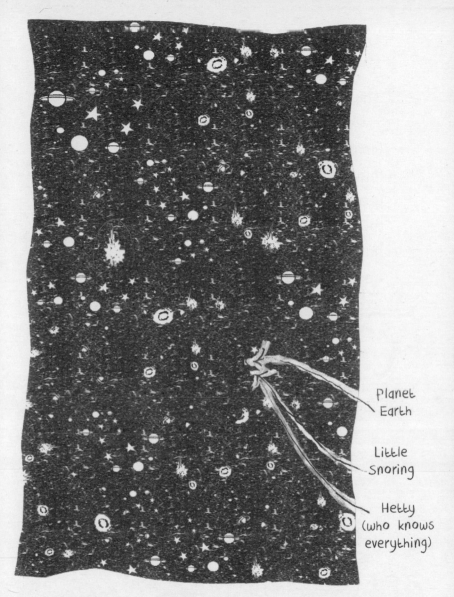

Planet
Earth

Little
Snoring

Hetty
(who knows
everything)

very small portion of the universe

was about to start shooting.

Once she had taken the register, Miss Green was even more displeased to discover that, as it was the last day of the school year and all the children hoped to audition that afternoon as extras for the movie, they had ants in their pants and were finding it hard to sit still.

(VERY IMPORTANT WARNING:
Please do not try putting ants in your pants at home, as some species of ant may bite even harder than my pet terrapin which has got a mean streak a mile wide and has a particularly nasty nip.)

 How many of these pants have aunts, I mean ants, in them?

18

Answer: All of them.

Tat had more ants in his pants than anybody else in the class. He didn't want to be in the movie, but he did want to find treasure. Over breakfast his dad, who was trying to earn some extra money helping to unload the equipment for the movie, had shown him the *Little Snoring Gazette* and the story that pointed to Captain Syd's lost treasure being buried in Little Snoring Castle. Definitely. Maybe.

Tat couldn't wait to start looking for it. He hoped the movie would give him a chance to get inside the castle, which was normally locked. He was determined to restore the Trout family fortunes which – as usual – were in a very bad way because although his dad had got his job back (part-time) as the lighthouse keeper, Tat and his little sister Tallulah's feet would keep on growing, which was very selfish of them. Having to buy new shoes was putting a strain on the family budget.

Tat looked at the maths questions and sighed loudly. He was of the opinion that there are only three kinds of people – those who can count and those who can't – and each time he added two numbers together

his brain gave a
squeal like a small
unhappy pig who
has just been
informed where
bacon comes from.
Every time he
squealed, Miss Green
glared at Tat.

Miss Green had been ever so much nicer to Tat – who was not very good at school subjects, but was very good at the things that really matter such as outwitting pirates, digging for treasure and swimming long distances – since he and Hetty had got rid of the Ghastly McNastys, and discovered all the lost shoes of Little Snoring. She had not just given him a superstar but also a certificate, which was

the first time that a member of the Trout family had received any kind of certificate since 1831 when Thomas William Ignatius Trout (otherwise known as TWIT) had been certified as being quite mad.

Mrs Trout proudly displayed the superstar and both certificates on the mantelpiece. They sat alongside a two-for-one offer for a miracle cream which stops feet smelling like stinky cheese (which she was going to get for Mr Trout, whose feet smelt like that kind of over-ripe Brie that is always trying to slide off the plate and make a dash for the door) and a money-off coupon for a holiday swimming with crocodiles.

Tat sighed. Over the last few weeks Miss Green had quite run out of superstars and niceness and she kept bursting into tears. As a result she had developed an almost permanent runny nose. She sat at her desk scrawling angrily across the children's homework – a project about spiders and their babies – with a red pen, while sniffing sadly.

(She and Mrs Slime, the McNastys' former second mate – reformed and regretful – who now lived in Little Snoring and helped out with reading once a week at the school, spent Sundays together taking it in turns to wipe their noses on each others' sleeves and trying to avoid falling over in the rising puddles of snot and tears which accumulated around their wellington boots. Mrs Slime's cold had improved enormously since she had stopped

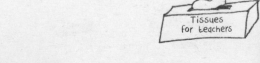

Sometimes Miss Green seemed so sad and angry that Tat felt he could see a real thundercloud above her head.

working for the McNastys and become friends with Tat and Hetty, but at the slightest sign of stress her nose gushed like a fast-flowing river.)

Tat could remember precisely when all Miss Green's niceness had been used up. It was on the very day, four weeks ago, when it had been announced that Little Snoring Castle was to be the location for the latest pirate movie – *Raiders of the Lost Shark* – being made by Bigwig Junior the Third, the famous hot-shot Hollywood film director. Hetty had brought the *Little Snoring Gazette* into class and read out the article to everyone. It said that the Caribbean had become far too expensive for pirate movies and that Little Snoring had been chosen instead because of its famous crumbling castle with its saltwater moat, perched right on the edge of the sea. Bigwig Junior didn't seem to be at all worried that Little Snoring Castle was damp, dank, dirty, dangerous, dingy and full of very hairy spiders the size of dinner plates. He loved spiders.

Hetty and Tat had thought that Miss Green, who was also fascinated by spiders, would be very excited to hear that a famous Hollywood movie director loved them too. All term she had been trying to get permission to take the children into the locked-up castle to study the castle spiders as part of their project on arachnids, but without success. She had even brought in a plan of the castle, which detailed all its rooms and its five hundred dank dungeons laid out over thirteen floors.

But when Hetty read out the newspaper article all the children became over-excited at

No, NOT kisses — crosses

Miss Green gives one tick for
every two thousand crosses.
(Hetty gets the tick.)

the prospect of playing extras in the movie, while Miss Green had just burst into tears.

They had been about to do chocolate finger painting, but Miss Green forgot about that and instead gave them a spelling test which included really difficult words like *really* and *difficult*.

Now, a month later, Tat progressed very slowly and painfully to question four of the maths problems. He was thinking about treasure. If the *Little Snoring Gazette* was correct, and Captain Syd's treasure was almost certainly definitely maybe buried in the castle, he hoped that the movie wouldn't get in the way of his trying to find it.

Tat's stomach rumbled. He remembered that he had a few jam sandwiches somewhere in the depths of his pocket. If he

picked the fluff off one of the sandwiches
and ate it without Mrs Green noticing, it
might give his brain the extra energy it
needed to struggle on to question five.

He rooted around in his pocket.

'What are you looking for?' hissed Hetty.

'The will to live,' said Tat gloomily.

Hetty grinned and squeezed his arm.
'You've only got to stay alive for the next
eleven minutes and nineteen seconds, Tat,'
she said soothingly, 'and then we're on our
summer holidays and we can start hunting
for treasure again. I've got a good feeling.
I just know that this time we'll find the
treasure.'

'Yes,' said Tat, who was sure that if Hetty
knew something it was almost certainly
true. 'And this time we won't have to worry
about the Ghastly McNastys getting their

grubby thieving hands on it because they are far away.' Triumphantly, Tat pulled a small fluff-covered packet out of his pocket and manoeuvred it onto his lap. It was full of strawberry-jam sandwiches – Tat's favourite – wrapped in an inside page of that morning's *Little Snoring Gazette*. The wrapping had come loose.

'What have you got there?' demanded Miss Green, eyeing Tat suspiciously. 'If it's a jam sandwich, Tat, I'm going to keep you in detention for the next six weeks. We will do triple arithmetic and double spelling together every single day without fail, and I will definitely make you spell very difficult words such as *definitely*, *abominable*, *budgerigar* and *crocodile*.'

Tat gulped. Everyone knew that *budgerigar* is hard to say and impossible to

spell unless you are a
superstar brainiac
genius like Hetty.

The quick-thinking
Hetty snatched the
sandwiches off his lap and promptly
sat on them. She felt the jam ooze down the
back of her legs. Hetty had landed herself
in a particularly sticky situation – but then
she had helped Tat out of a sticky situation,
and helping each other out of sticky
situations is the reason we have friends.

'Come here, Tat,' said Miss Green
ominously. 'Bring whatever you've got in
your hand with you. I've warned you
before. There are three things that I will not
stand in my classroom: imagination,
reading for pleasure, and jam sandwiches.
They are all simply frightful for attracting

31

the wasps.' She held out her hand. Tat gave her the slightly sticky newspaper. The headline shouted:

## EXCLUSIVE!
## BIGWIG JUNIOR THE THIRD
## ARRIVES IN LITTLE SNORING.

There was a large picture of a smiling Bigwig Junior the Third who was quoted as saying, 'Raiders of the Lost Shark *is going*

*to be the biggest and best pirate movie ever made. Even sharks will be selling their teeth to the tooth fairy for a ticket. All those who want to be extras should come dressed as pirates to Little Snoring Castle this afternoon for auditions. Please don't worry about the spiders, we have removed them to a safe place – all except one the size of a cartwheel which got away but is probably harmless provided nobody upsets it.'*

Miss Green stared at the headline and picture and looked very sad. 'Class dismissed,' she shouted, and the children cheered and headed for the exit, delighted that their summer was beginning at last.

At the door, Tat glanced back. A bedraggled parrot had alighted on the windowsill and Miss Green was absent-mindedly feeding it one of the squashed jam sandwiches that Hetty had sat on. A tear was running down Miss Green's cheek.

Even though Miss Green had been horrid to him, Tat had a kind heart and he couldn't help but feel sorry for her. He wondered what was making her so very unhappy.

# Chapter 3

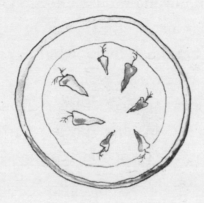

Tat and Hetty were at Tat's house eating their lunch. It was a small lunch because the Trout family did not have very much money. Only that morning at breakfast Mrs Trout had announced to her husband, Tat,

Tallulah, Dog (who was actually a cat but behaved just like a dog) and the mouse that lived under the skirting board, that what the Trouts desperately needed was a family budget. Tat was trying to share out seven small carrots between four of them which was very difficult, but much more useful than any of the sums that Miss Green set.

'Oh dear me, no,' said Mrs Trout when she saw Tat dividing the last carrot. 'I'm afraid we can't eat that carrot. We must leave it for your dad — he will be very hungry after a morning on the harbour helping to unload all the equipment for the movie, and the tank of sharks. Your dad says they are going to let the sharks loose in the moat tomorrow morning.'

She saw Tat tighten his belt and her face

fell. 'I'm so sorry, Tat. I feel such a failure, but at all costs we really must avoid running into debt again.'

'Please don't worry, Mrs Trout,' said Hetty kindly. 'Tat and I are going treasure hunting this afternoon at the castle, so maybe the Trout family fortunes will be restored by tea time.'

'I do hope so,' said Tallulah, 'because then we can have ring doughnuts for tea. For the last three weeks we've only been able to have the hole in the middle.'

The door opened and Mr Trout came in, looking exhausted. He had a bird on his shoulder.

'What's that?' demanded Mrs Trout.

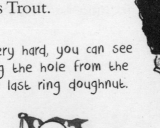

If you look very hard, you can see Tallulah holding the hole from the middle of her last ring doughnut.

Mr Trout smiled. 'It's a budgie, of course, my dear. This morning at breakfast you said that what the Trouts desperately needed was a family budgie. So I got us one. Found it in the pet shop going cheap.'

Mrs Trout stared at her husband impatiently. 'Are you deaf?' she asked sharply.

'No, I'm Mr Trout,' he replied, puzzled. He really thought his wife should know who he was, as they had been married for fifteen years and had two children together.

'Budget. I said we needed a budget, not a budgie,' snapped Mrs Trout, even though she rarely snapped at her husband because she loved him dearly. 'A budgie is another mouth to feed.'

'The budgie can have my carrot,' said Mr Trout quietly, and he looked so stricken at his mistake that Mrs Trout leapt from her chair guiltily and hugged him.

'Actually,' said Hetty, looking at the bedraggled bird, 'that's not a budget *or* a budgie.'

They all turned to her.

'That is Pegleg Polly,' said Hetty, 'the Ghastly McNastys' parrot.'

'Nasty boys! Porky pies!' squawked Pegleg Polly. It had been Pegleg Polly who pulled the plug on the McNastys' ship, *The Rotten Apple*, causing it to sink. She had been furious at being sucked into the belly of the whale alongside the twins. She had felt sick as a parrot the whole time because the twins behaved very badly towards her. Every time she fell asleep they had tried to catch her and turn her into parrot burgers.

The McNastys seemed to have no idea that eating your pets is quite, quite wrong.

Pegleg Polly was delighted to be rid of the McNastys. She looked mournfully at Mrs Trout.

'Pretty Polly, hungry Polly,' she said hopefully. Polly was always hungry.

Mrs Trout smiled. 'What's one more mouth?' she said. 'I'll just have to redo the family budget to include the budgie, or rather parrot. She can stay. Give that poor hungry bird the last carrot.'

Pegleg Polly flew across the room and gave Mrs Trout an affectionate peck on the cheek.

'Ah, love at first bite,' said Mr Trout,

looking at this touching scene and trying
not to think about the hole in his tummy.

(Important! Please note: Mr Trout did not
actually have a hole in his stomach, which
would be a medical emergency because all
his insides would fall out onto the floor
and make a terrible mess. It is merely a
turn of phrase indicating that Mr Trout
was so hungry he could eat a horse,
although Mr Trout loved horses and would
never ever dream of trying to eat one.
Unlike the McNastys, who would eat
anything except boiled hippopotamus, all
green vegetables and yak's milk pudding. I
have tried yak's milk pudding myself so
that you don't have to, and I can assure
you that it makes anyone who tastes it
screw up their face and go 'Yak!')

'Come on,' said Tat, jumping to his feet. 'Let's go treasure hunting.'

Dog jumped up with excitement, wagged his tail furiously and meowed loudly. Dog loved digging for things, particularly old shoes and treasure. Pegleg Polly flew from her perch on top of the kitchen dresser and landed on Tat's shoulder.

'Yes, you must come too, Polly,' said Tat. A strange look came over his face.

'What's wrong, Tat?' asked Mrs Trout, wondering if Tat was coming down with the measles. 'Are you ill?'

'No,' said Tat, 'I've just had a thought.'

The Trout family stared at him anxiously. Thoughts could be such dangerous things. You never knew where they might lead.

'If Pegleg Polly is here in Little Snoring, then maybe the McNastys are here too. If they are, then they'll be looking for Captain Syd's treasure.'

'Clever boy. This Trout is not a twit,' squawked Polly excitedly.

'You're right, Tat,' said Hetty admiringly.

'We're going to have to keep our eyes peeled for them.'

NB Do NOT try peeling your eyes. They are not potatoes.

'We may have to do more than that,' said Tat. 'We need to lure them into a trap.'

'But we'll have to find them first,' said Hetty.

Tat nodded. 'That's easy peasy. Sooner or later they'll hear that Captain Syd's treasure may be buried at the castle. When they do, they'll head straight there to get their greedy hands on it.'

'You are clever,' said Hetty.

Tat blushed. 'Let's go treasure hunting and pirate hunting!'

'Let's,' agreed Hetty, 'but let's go prepared.' She reached for a sheet of paper and started to draw a treasure map.

That is quite enough of Chapter 3.

# Chapter 4

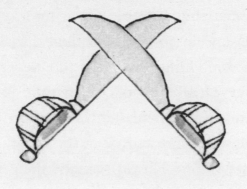

The Ghasty McNastys were dismayed to discover that there was a long queue of people dressed as pirates outside the castle. They didn't realise that they had all come to audition to be extras in *Raiders of the Lost*

*Shark*. They thought they were all real – but oddly well-behaved – pirates, also seeking the treasure.

In fact, with the exception of Tat and Hetty, the Little Snoring villagers had long ago lost interest in the treasure, which despite the continuous rumours and pronouncements from experts that it was buried in Little Snoring, had never been found. They were all much more excited about finding fame as extras in a Hollywood movie.

But the McNastys thought they had to get into the castle before everyone else and

A present from the McNastys

FLEAS (fresh)

find the treasure first. They certainly didn't want to have to share it – the McNastys hated sharing anything, except their nits and fleas, which they did their best to give to everyone.

They elbowed their way through the crowd, knocking the pirate hats off several old ladies and stamping on the toes of every single child from the Greater Snoring Stage School for Little Brats and Terrible Show-offs and making them cry and get hiccups so they had to go home and stand on their heads (which, as everybody knows, is the

AUDITIONS →

best cure for hiccups). The McNastys made their way over the drawbridge and under the portcullis, barged to the front of the queue, and were about to step through the castle door when their way was barred by a man with a moustache.

'Are you here for the auditions?' he demanded.

'No, we're here for the treasure,' said Captain Gruesome.

Grisly kicked him. Maybe this man didn't know about the treasure. The fewer people who knew about the treasure, the better.

'I'm afraid the castle is closed to everyone except those auditioning to play extras in the blockbuster movie *Raiders of the Lost Shark*,' said the man.

The McNastys tried to push past him,

 Another present from the McNastys

but he stopped them. 'You can't come in. My word is law! Smell my feet!'

SMELL MY FEET!

Captain Gruesome thought it an odd request but he had always found the aroma of rubbish tips and smelly feet oddly alluring.

He began to bend down, but Captain

Grisly turned to the man and said nastily, 'You are such a bossypants!'

'How did you know my name?' demanded the man, who really was called Mr Bossypants. He was Bigwig Junior the Third's personal assistant, and he certainly lived up to his name. He bossed Bigwig Junior around – he'd even ordered him to break off his engagement once, saying love and marriage would get in the way of his art, but that was because Mr Bossypants was secretly jealous of Bigwig.

(Bigwig Junior the Third had been living unhappily ever after, because he had really loved his fiancée and had dreamt of marrying her, retiring from the movie business and moving to Little Snoring.)

Captain Gruesome realised that if he wanted to get into the castle, he was either

going to have to cut off
Mr Bossypants's nose
with his cutlass or flatter
him. He decided that
flattery was less fun
but less bloody too.

'We know your
name because
*everyone* has heard
of Mr Bossypants.
Your name is famed
far and wide at the
Royal Sharkspeare
Company, where my
brother and I have
been acting and
winning awards for
the last few years.
They are in awe of you.'

'The Royal Sharkspeare Company,' said Mr Bossypants, looking impressed. He had never heard of the Royal Sharkspeare Company but it must be a truly wonderful theatre company if they had heard of him.

'You must be great friends with those directors, John Dory and Jack Spratt?' said Captain Gruesome.

'Oh, of course,' gushed Mr Bossypants, although he had never heard of them either.

'The best of their generation,' said Captain Gruesome. 'They directed me when I gave my famous performance as Haddock, Prince of Denmark.' He bowed low. 'We are the McLuvvies. At your service and always in the service of art.'

'Darlings, how absolutely marvellous. So authentic the way you've dressed for the audition.

More presents from the McNastys

Only true artists would go to such trouble.'
Mr Bossypants sniffed. There was a strange
smell of maggotty fish hanging around the
McLuvvies, but he guessed it must be their
way of getting into character. 'You're in luck.
This morning two of the actors playing
pirates had to be sacked from the shoot. They
claimed to have seen two pirates, a parrot
and a teddy bear flying through the air.
What nonsense! So I'm sure that I can get
Biggiewiggie to give you their roles. You'll
just have to do a little audition to show him
how brilliantly you both act.'

They followed him into the castle,
delighted to have got inside.

'Squeaky pants! I don't know how to
act,' hissed Captain Grisly.

'You won't have to,' whispered
Captain Gruesome.

Even more
presents from
the McNastys

53

'You are auditioning to play a pirate and you are a pirate. And you're not actually going to act in the movie – you'll be too busy looking for the treasure. But if we get cast, we'll have free run of the castle and can go where we like and find the treasure before anyone else.'

# Chapter 5

Tat, Hetty, Dog and Pegleg Polly looked at the long queue outside the castle. At this rate it would be the end of the summer holidays before they got inside. When Hetty had seen the queue of people waiting to audition, she had said thoughtfully, 'I wonder if the McNastys are here? They would be hard to spot because everyone is dressed like pirates. We really are going to have to be on the lookout for them.'

They went to talk to their friend, Mrs Slime, who was standing in the queue. Her cold was so much better since she had left the McNastys' employment that she only needed five boxes of tissues a day.

'Is Miss Green okay?' asked Tat, who knew the two women were good friends and was worried about his teacher.

Mrs Slime shook her head sadly. 'Poor woman, she's in a bad way. She can't stop crying. I only wish I knew why. But she won't say. If we could just think of a way to cheer her up.'

Can you spot the McNastys?

There was a sudden commotion at the front of the queue.

'Look!' said Hetty urgently. 'It's the McNastys trying to barge their way into the castle. You were right, Tat. They must be here to look for the treasure and grab it for themselves.'

'You must stop them,' said Mrs Slime.

'We intend to,' said Tat, triumphantly producing the treasure map that Hetty had drawn from his pocket. After being in Tat's pocket for a couple of hours the map now looked centuries old. 'We're going to use it to lure the McNastys into a deep, dark dungeon – dungeon 244 – and lock them in while we try and find the treasure.'

'Clever idea,' said Mrs Slime approvingly. 'I'll come with you and help.'

But getting into the castle proved a

problem. Just when they thought they were about to succeed, the bossy little man with a moustache so small and shiny that it looked as if a slug had taken up residence on his top lip returned to the door and barred their way.

'Go away, horrible children, go away. The talented performing infants from the Greater Snoring Stage School for Little Brats and Terrible Show-offs are coming to play the children's roles. We don't need any more repulsive children.'

He looked at Pegleg Polly with disgust. 'Or that pathetic excuse for

# Bossy Knickers!

a parrot. We've got wooden parrots. They always turn in much better performances.' Pegleg Polly looked quite crestfallen.

Dog and Polly had struck up quite a friendship. Unseen, Dog cocked his leg against the man. A trickle ran down Mr Bossypants's leg. He didn't notice – he was too busy sneering at Mrs Slime and her nose, which had begun to run rather a lot because of the stress.

'GO AWAY! Do you not know who I am? I am the famed Mr Bossypants, personal assistant to Bigwig Junior the Third. My word is law. Smell my feet!'

They certainly didn't want to do that, and

in any case Mr Bossypants slammed the
castle door in their faces, which lightly
grazed the end of all their noses and Pegleg
Polly's beak.

'What are we going to do now?' asked Tat.

'I wonder if castles have back doors?' said
Hetty.

'Not all of them, dear,' said Mrs Slime.
'But this one does.'

They walked around the other side of

the castle. Across the moat they could see a closed drawbridge. But even if they could get across the moat, they wouldn't be able to get the drawbridge down as it would be locked from the inside of the castle.

'Wait a minute,' said Tat suddenly. 'I could swim across the moat.'

'You could,' said Hetty, who knew that Tat was a champion swimmer. 'But we still wouldn't be able to open the drawbridge.'

Tat looked at Pegleg Polly who was lying on the ground, relaxing. 'If Polly could fly over the walls and undo the bolts with her beak, maybe I could lever the

drawbridge down and then the rest of you could come across.'

'Clever Tat! Not a twit!' squawked Pegleg Polly.

'Wait,' said Hetty. 'I thought they were going to put sharks in the moat for the movie.'

'They are,' said Tat. 'But only when they start filming tomorrow. Look – there are no sharks now.' He felt in his pocket and dropped a jam sandwich in the moat. They were mobbed by a family of ducks, but there was no sign of any sharks.

'Let's do it,' said Hetty. She grinned at her friend. 'You are brave as well as clever, Tat.'

So Tat swam across the moat, and Pegleg Polly flew over the ramparts and pulled back the bolts on either side of the drawbridge. Tat found an old iron bar on the grass and inserted it into the side of the drawbridge and it crashed open easily. If Tat hadn't jumped swiftly out of the way he

This is what 60 pots of Tat jam would look like (three of them would probably have broken, and four would have been eaten).

would have been completely squashed and could have been turned into 67 pots of jam.

They headed straight down to the dungeons. The film people were busy and fortunately took little notice of them, assuming they were extras. The dungeons were dark, dank, dirty, dangerous and dingy and Tat was shivering hard after his swim.

'My teeth won't stop ch-ch-ch-ch-chattering,' he whispered to Hetty.

'I just hope they're saying something interesting,' said Hetty. She handed him the

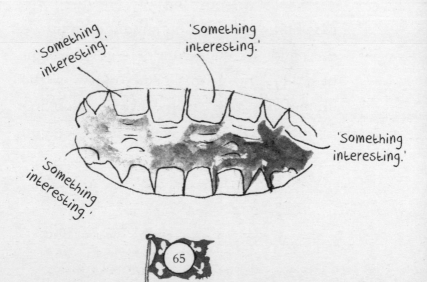

'Something interesting.'

'Something interesting.'

'Something interesting.'

'Something interesting.'

sweater she had tied around her waist. He put it on gratefully.

They were deciding which way to go when they heard a voice (which is not at all surprising – you would only be surprised if you saw a voice).

'Hey! You children! This way, this way.' The man was smiling and he looked nice. He held out his hand.

'I'm Bigwig Junior the Third and I'm the director of *Raiders of the Lost Shark*. You must be the children from the Greater Snoring Stage School for Little Brats and Terrible Show-offs and . . .' He turned to Mrs Slime. '. . . and you, madam, must be the children's chaperone.' He caught sight of Polly and Dog. 'These must be the animal extras we ordered. I've been looking for you everywhere. We need to get you into your costumes so that we can rehearse the scene and then we can shoot you tomorrow.'

Pegleg Polly gave a frightened squawk. She didn't want to be shot tomorrow. In fact she didn't want to be shot at all. Even the Ghastly McNastys had never suggested shooting her. She hopped about anxiously on Tat's shoulder until Hetty explained that shooting a movie didn't involve anyone getting killed.

Tat and Hetty had met the children from Greater Snoring Stage School for Little Brats and Terrible Show-offs on their way to the castle. They had all been crying and hiccupping and vowing never to return, so they knew that they wouldn't be coming back. Tat and Hetty looked at each other. They had been so focused on finding the treasure, they hadn't thought about being in the movie. But Hetty loved acting and Tat had always fancied having a real go at it, but Miss Green would never give him a proper part in school plays. When they had done a Nativity play, Tat had been cast as the manger. The critic from the *Little Snoring Gazette* had been very complimentary – she said she had never seen a performance quite so wooden.

'Actually,' said Tat shyly, 'we're not from the Greater Snoring Stage School for Little Brats and Terrible Show-offs, but we'll give it a go.'

'Splendid,' said Bigwig who felt quite

relieved. These children seemed delightful, and they wouldn't have to do much – just dress up as little pirates, look fierce and go 'Arrrgh' a great deal. 'Well if you are prepared to step in at such short notice, I would be very grateful. In fact I'm so grateful I'll not only pay you the going rate but throw in unlimited ring doughnuts, too.'

'Would the ring doughnuts include the entire doughnut or would it just be the hole?' asked Tat.

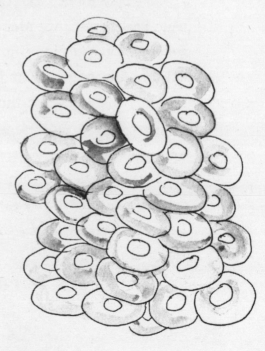

Bigwig looked shocked. 'Of course it would be the whole thing. The hole alone is hardly worth the effort. And you can have the run of the castle to play in, as long as you are not scared of spiders.'

'We love spiders,' said Hetty. 'We did a school project on them.'

'Good. But do keep a lookout for the great big hairy spider the size of a cartwheel. I'd love to see it myself, but no luck yet. It's very rare and it could be very friendly too, but we can't be completely sure. So if you spot it, whatever you do, don't do anything to upset it, because we can't afford to lose any more of the cast.'

It was too good an offer for the children to turn down. Bigwig held out his hand and they all shook it (including Dog and Polly), and then he took them to the

costume department, which was
like the biggest dressing-up box in
the world. But the children didn't
have time to stop and play – they
were on a mission to find the world's
ghastliest and nastiest pirates and find
Captain Syd's lost treasure too.

Tat, Hetty, Dog and Polly were in
dungeon 433, looking for treasure and the
McNastys. So far they had found neither.
They had begun pirate- and treasure-
hunting in dungeon 500, which was in
the deepest and darkest part of the castle,
and were working their way back to
dungeon number one. They were fuelled
by a large bag of ring doughnuts given to
them by Bigwig Junior the Third. Polly

had eaten most of them.

'There's nothing here,' said Hetty. 'Let's look in the next dungeon.'

They were about to leave when Tat spotted something in a crack in the darkest, deepest, dingiest corner of the dungeon. He put his hand into the crack and to his intense excitement found a secret lever. He pulled it and the crack in the wall opened wider.

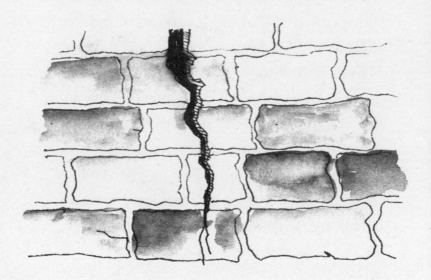

'Look what I've found!' he shouted to the others.

There were gasps of astonishment.

'Don't touch!' warned Mrs Slime, whose nose had begun to run even faster with the excitement.

Hetty, Mrs Slime, Dog and Polly all stared open-mouthed. They had never seen anything so wondrous.

Then Tat pulled the lever again and the space closed up. They knew that what they had found was so precious they had to keep it safe.

'Mrs Slime,' Tat said urgently, 'do you think you could go and tell Miss Green what we've found? I'm certain it would make her feel a little better.'

Mrs Slime smeezed (which is a cross between a smile and a sneeze). 'I'll do better

Hee hee choo!

This is the sound a smeeze makes.

than that, Tat. I'll bring her back to the castle so she can see the treasure you've found herself. You are a clever, kind boy, Tat. But make sure you watch out for those ghastly, nasty pirates while I'm gone.'

'We will,' said Tat. 'But so far we've been looking for them without success.'

Dog meowed loudly.

Tat ignored him. Dog meowed louder and put his nose to the ground and sniffed around. Polly squawked encouragement. Dog meowed louder and moved towards the door.

'Maggotty fish?' asked Tat. Dog nodded and wagged his tail happily. Tat and Hetty looked at each other.

'Oh Dog, you are the cleverest cat in the world,' said Hetty. 'Lead us to the McNastys, and the biggest bone you can carry home from the butcher's will be yours.'

There is no Chapter 6 because it ran off the page.

# Chapter 7

Dog led the children up the spiral staircase and along a gloomy corridor on the ground floor of the castle. He was following a smell of maggotty fish. It was getting stronger. They passed a large room with a big baronial fireplace where a fire was laid but not lit. There was no sign of the McNastys inside, but there were two chairs. On the back of one, in small writing, it said: *Bigwig: director*. On the other, in much bigger writing, it said: **Bossypants: VIP**. There was also a large props table full of pirate-related items.

'This must be Bigwig's office, where he's holding the auditions,' said Hetty.

Suddenly they heard voices. Two of the voices belonged to Bigwig and Mr Bossypants and the other two unmistakeably belonged to the McNastys. All four voices were coming in their direction.

'The map!' hissed Hetty. 'Hide it where the McNastys are likely to spot it. Not too obvious or they'll realise it's a fake, but not so hard that they don't find it.'

Tat looked wildly around, then he ran to the great fireplace, looked up the chimney and stuck the map into a gap in the brickwork. Then he, Hetty, Dog and Polly hid behind the heavy brocade curtains as the four men entered the room. Captain Grisly was cackling, 'Those sharks were real beauties. I've never seen sleeker creatures or sharper teeth.'

As soon as they had heard about the sharks, the McNastys had demanded to be taken to see them in the great tank situated in a room under the moat. They called them 'my pretties' and teased them terribly by holding Captain Grisly's terrified teddy bear up to the glass and shouting, 'Come and get your dinner.' They were thrilled when Mr Bossypants showed them the

secret button which, when it was pushed, opened specially installed glass panels in the top of the tank, allowing the sharks to swim out into the moat.

Teddy said nothing about his ill-treatment — because he couldn't talk — but he was plotting his revenge on the Ghastly McNastys.

# Teddy's Revenge

Lure McNastys into a **PiT** filled with

## CENSORED

← Sorry, not suitable for under 18s

Bigwig Junior the Third and Mr Bossypants sat down in the chairs and the McNastys wandered around the room examining the props and looking up the chimney.

All the clever-cloggy brainiacs amongst you can try this fiendishly difficult quiz: Captain Gruesome was looking up the chimney because:

1) He liked the smell of soot and was thinking of using it as a secret ingredient in a new perfume range for pirates called Pong. (Existing perfumes included: Dung, Poo and Stinkerama.)

2) He wanted to see if it was possible to spot the blue sky at the very top.

3) He hoped to find a stash of hidden treasure.

4) He very kindly wanted to rescue all small Victorian sweeps who had become stuck up chimneys and return them to their desolate mothers.

5) He was looking for a sooty albatross. The sooty albatross is a shy bird and if you are very shy and very sooty a chimney is a good place to hide if you don't want to meet people, although you do have to watch out for singed feathers.

(You can find the answer on page 126.)

Hetty winked at Tat as they spied Captain Gruesome reaching up the chimney for something and putting it in his pocket along with several other things he'd swiped from the props table when he thought Bigwig and Mr Bossypants weren't looking.

'Eh, shall we begin the audition,' said Mr Bossypants, clapping his hands together. The McNastys glared at him. They made people walk the plank for less than clapping their hands. Then they remembered: if they got through the dratted audition, they would have free run of the castle.

They were both fed up at wasting their time with all this acting business when they could be looking for treasure. They glared at Bigwig and Mr Bossypants and started

waving their cutlasses around menacingly.

Peeping from behind the brocade curtain, Tat could see Bigwig cowering under his chair like a wet sock.

'Do we get the parts?' enquired the twins. There was only one possible answer to this question.

'Yes,' said Bigwig weakly. 'You're cast. Mr Bossypants will show you the way to the costume department in the dungeons. But do watch out for the spider. It's roaming around down there somewhere.'

'Spider!' said the McNastys, and suddenly they looked a little less fearsome.

'You're not afraid of a spider, are you?' asked Bigwig.

The McNastys waved their cutlasses ominously.

'We are afraid of nothing,' they cried, which wasn't entirely true as they were often really, really scared when they looked at themselves in the mirror and both of them hated spiders. 'Anyone who says we are afraid of spiders will be made to walk the plank.'

'I won't say anything then,' said Bigwig faintly, mopping the sweat off his brow.

'Darlings, you were marvellous,' gushed Mr Bossypants. The McNastys pushed him aside, delighted that they now had the run of the castle and could look for Captain Syd's treasure without being challenged. They grinned nastily and left the room. But the fleas they had brought with them didn't – they much preferred Mr Bossypants's expensive silk suit to the McNastys' threadbare rags.

'What a lucky find they are,' said Mr Bossypants. 'They are both terrifyingly good. I'm prepared to bet big money that they will win Oscars for their performances.'

Mr Bossypants reached for his wallet. He patted all his pockets but mysteriously it seemed to have gone missing. Suddenly he scratched under his armpit – he was feeling very itchy. He stalked off to look for his wallet and take a shower.

As soon as he had gone, the children emerged from behind the curtain. Bigwig smiled when he saw them.

'What are you doing here?'

'We've got something important to tell you,' said Hetty. 'The good news is that we've found something very precious that we want to show you, but the bad news is that those two actors you've just hired for your movie are not actors at all. They are the McNastys, who are the nastiest pirates ever to have sailed the Seven Seas.'

'Oh dear,' said Bigwig, 'I fear that could be very bad news for all of us.'

'It would be,' said Tat, 'but Hetty and I

are confident that any minute now the McNastys will be heading for dungeon 244 and when they walk inside, we'll slam the door and lock them in so they can't harm anybody.'

The Ghastly McNastys were hiding in one of the dungeons and emptying their pockets of all the things they had stolen so far, which included Mr Bossypants's wallet and several props that they had found lying around – only they hadn't realised that they were props. They were very disappointed to discover that the

gold ducats were foil-wrapped chocolate, although they gobbled them down greedily and so fast that they both burped 116 times which they thought might be a world record and their greatest achievement in life so far.

BUUUUUUURRP
BURP! BURP burp BURP
(Belch) BURRP Buuurp
BURP Burrp burp BURPBURP
Burp BURP burp BURP! Burp
BUURP burp BURP burp BURP
BURP BURP! BURP! Burp
BurpBurp burp BURP Burp
BURP! Burrrp BURP! BURP
BURP! BURP! BURP! Burp
BURP BURP BURP!
BURP BURP! Burp BURP
BURP! Burp BURP

Burp BURP! BURP burp
BURRRP
BUUUUUUURRP
BURP! BURP burp BURP
(Belch) BURRP Buuurp
BURP Burrp
burp BURPBURP
Burp BURP burp BURP! Burp
BUURP burp BURP burp BURP
BURP BURP! BURP! burp
BURPBurp burp BURP Burp
BURP! Burrrp BURP! BURP
BURP! BURP! BURP! Burp
BURP Burp BURP!
BURP BURP! Burp BURP
BURP! Burp BURP
Buuuurp! BURP! Burp
BURRP! BURP Burp
Buuurp BURP Buuurp!
BURP BURP!

There was only one thing left to look at: a rolled up bit of paper that Captain Gruesome had found tucked up inside the enormous chimney in the room where they had auditioned.

Captain Gruesome unfurled the paper excitedly. It was as crumbly as mouldy cheese. Gruesome screwed up his eyes.

'Sweaty socks!' he cried in triumph. 'We've found the map which marks the spot where Captain Syd's treasure is buried. It is in dungeon 244 which is a deep, dark, dingy dungeon directly below this one.'

'Squeaky pants! We'll be rich!' said Captain Grisly.

'I'm a clever clogs for finding it,' said Gruesome. 'The cleverest, craftiest, most cunning clever clogs the world has ever seen. Ouch!' Grisly had pinched him very hard.

'Why did you do that?' asked Gruesome grumpily.

'Because I'm cleverer and craftier than you,' said Grisly.

'You're not,' roared Gruesome. 'You are a dull-witted, bird-brained, muttonhead.'

Gruesome pinched his brother who pinched him back and soon they were rolling around on the floor biffing and boffing each other as hard as they could.

They were so busy that they didn't notice that the treasure map had fallen onto the floor and floated across on a draught through the open door of the dungeon. They didn't notice or hear the approach of Mrs Slime and Miss Green, who were on their way to dungeon 433.

It had taken all her powers of persuasion for Mrs Slime to get Miss

Green to the castle and in the end she had been quite sharp with her friend and told her that she should stop wallowing in her misery and come and see what her clever pupils had found.

They had made quite slow progress to the castle because Miss Green kept stopping to have a little cry, which Mrs Slime found very stressful and which only made her sneeze more and more. By the time they reached the back door of the castle she had already used up all her tissues. They were creeping past the dungeon where the McNastys were fighting, when they were forced to stop by the imminent approach of one of Mrs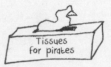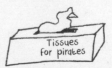

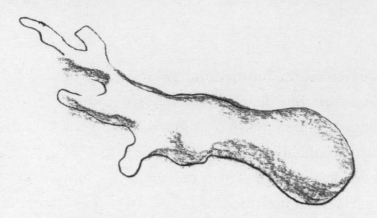

Slime's explosive sneezes. Mrs Slime knew she needed to take prompt action to avert a snot disaster. She looked wildly around. They had no tissues, sleeves or socks left to stop the tide of slime or the noise that might alert the McNastys to their presence. She spied the parchment on the floor. It was totally inadequate, but it would have to do. She glanced briefly at it, and then there was a noise as loud as a cannon as she sneezed into it.

The McNastys stopped fighting and looked up, just in time to see their precious treasure map disintegrate into a pulp of green slime. They suddenly realised that although they had looked at the map, they hadn't actually made a mental note of what it said and where the treasure could be found in the castle.

The McNastys grabbed Mrs Slime and Miss Green and held them tight even when Mrs Slime sneezed all over them, which Captain Gruesome thought was actually refreshing as he had been feeling quite hot.

The McNastys were furious at the loss of their treasure map and they flipped like angry pancakes, which was a truly terrifying sight. If you have ever seen an angry pancake you will know quite how terrifying that is. It is infinitely worse than seeing ten hungry cannibals running

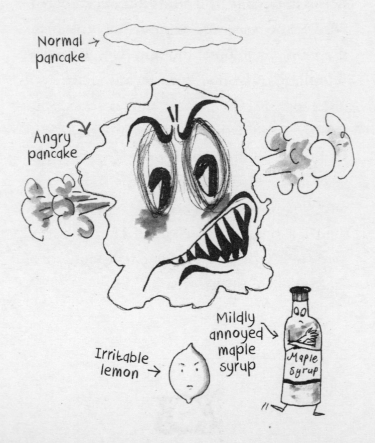

Normal → pancake

Angry pancake

Irritable lemon →

Mildly annoyed maple syrup

Maple syrup

towards you with their arms and mouths wide open, or discovering that the bridge you are using to cross the river is made from seventeen cunning crocodiles with very sharp teeth.

Fortunately, Miss Green was a teacher and she had seen far more terrifying sights in her life, including an entire over-tired Reception class trying to learn to tie their shoelaces.

'Oh, do stop flipping immediately,' ordered Miss Green. She said it so sternly that it reminded the McNastys of being told off at Pirate School and they stopped, fell silent and simply glared at Miss Green and Mrs Slime. They hated Mrs Slime who they felt had betrayed them. They loomed over the two women menacingly and gave them their most threatening stare.

'Sweaty socks! We're going to have to tie you up and shine a very bright torch in your eyes and ask you very difficult questions before we throw you to the sharks,' said Captain Gruesome. He suddenly felt surprisingly happy.

'Squeaky pants! It's a dastardly delightful day for ghastliness,' said Captain Grisly, 'and we are going to be very ghastly to you.'

'Yes, we're going to have to get tough

with you. Really tough,' said Captain Gruesome. 'And when you are quaking with terror you will give us all the information we want from you.'

Miss Green didn't look in the slightest bit worried. 'What information is that?' she asked. Despite her misery, when faced with danger Miss Green went into automatic teacher-mode. She sat down on a ledge and patted either side of her. 'Why don't you come and sit down, and I'll tell you everything you want to know.'

The twins looked at each other. It really was very hard to disobey Miss Green because she was a teacher, and

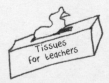

everybody finds it hard to disobey teachers, even nasty pirates.

'Here,' she said, talking to the McNastys as if they were small children in her nursery class. 'One of you sit on my left hand and one of you sit on my right hand.'

The McNastys were puzzled. They weren't very good at their lefts and their rights and they had no idea why Miss Green wanted them to sit on her hands, but like lots of people when faced with a teacher, they were too nervous to disobey. She really was very stern and, besides, it would stop her running away.

'Ouch!' said Miss Green and bit her lip as the McNastys sat heavily on each of her hands. It was very painful. She slid her hands out from under their nasty stinky bottoms as quickly as she could.

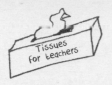

'Now,' she said, smiling, which took a great deal of effort because the whiff from the McNastys' clothes and the pong from their unbrushed teeth was quite over-powering, 'how can we help you?'

'Tell us the spot where X was marked on the map Mrs Slime sneezed all over and which is now a slimy pulp,' asked Captain Gruesome.

'Oh, that's easy,' said Miss Green pleasantly. She winked at Mrs Slime. 'I looked before I sneezed.' She thought of a number entirely at random. 'X marks the spot in dungeon 433. I am right, Mrs Slime, am I not?'

'You are always right, Miss Green,' said Mrs Slime. Then she suddenly realised that the number that Miss Green had said just happened to be the actual number of the

dungeon where the precious treasure was
hidden, so she added hastily, 'except when
you are wrong. It's not that dungeon, it's —'

But it was too late. The McNastys knew
that they just had to go to dungeon 433
and the treasure would be theirs.

But first they grabbed Miss Green and

Mrs Slime, and pushed them into the dungeon (which happened to be number 53), slammed the door and turned the key in the lock. They couldn't allow them to go free in case they raised the alarm that there were two real pirates loose in the castle.

'You'll not escape from here, and just to make sure I'm taking the key with me,' chuckled Captain Gruesome, pocketing it.

Then the McNastys hurried away to look for the treasure.

Inside the dark, dingy, damp dungeon, Mrs Slime began to sneeze. The shock brought her cold back with a vengeance. Miss Green began to cry great fat tears that formed a pool at her feet. Her nose began to run too. Neither of them had anything on which to blow their noses. The puddle of snotty, salty, sticky slime around their feet began to get higher. Very soon it was nearly up to their waists and rising fast.

'I think,' said Mrs Slime bravely, 'we are in what is known as a sticky situation.'

This page is 110 and it is one of my favourite pages in this entire book, if not the entire universe. It is not blank. It is full of something awesome. You will just have to search very very very hard to find it. This will be done most successfully with your eyes shut and using your imagination (but do please watch out for wasps which are strongly attracted to imagination).

# Chapter 8

Tat, Hetty, Dog and Polly were in dungeon 433 showing Bigwig what they had found. They then planned to go to dungeon 244 where they were sure the McNastys would be looking for the treasure.

'Well that's amazing,' said Bigwig as Tat pressed the hidden lever so the crack in the wall closed.

'Amazing,' agreed Hetty. 'We couldn't believe our luck when we found it.'

The McNastys were making their way along the corridor and heard what Hetty was saying. They looked at each other (which was quite unpleasant and frightening for both of them). Those horrible children, Tat and Hetty, must have discovered the treasure. They rushed into the dungeon, hands outstretched, ready to gather up all the emeralds and gold bars and diamonds that they were sure were there.

'Oh no! It's the Ghastly McNastys!' cried Hetty.

'Everyone hates us,' Captain Gruesome roared.

'Don't be ridiculous,' retorted Captain Grisly, 'not everyone has met us yet.' He paused and then added boldly, 'But when they do, they will.'

'That's because we are so ghastly and nasty,' said Captain Gruesome proudly, 'and we are about to be very ghastly and nasty to you horrible, hideous children, that disgusting cat called Dog and that total disgrace of a one-legged parrot, unless you immediately hand over all the treasure you've just found.'

They looked around greedily. They could see no sign of sparkling jewels or piles of silver. They decided that the children must have stuffed it all in their pockets. They took a step towards them and waved their cutlasses very threateningly at Bigwig, who had his hands outstretched and was trying to be very brave and protect the children even though both his knees were knocking together.

'Run!' shouted Tat, and he quickly pelted the McNastys with ring doughnuts. Tat's aim

was very true
and several
doughnuts caught
on the McNastys'
noses so they
looked like a living
hoopla stall at a
funfair. Although it
wasn't very fun for
the McNastys
whose faces got
very sugary
and sticky.
The children
and Bigwig took
the opportunity to
slip by the
surprised
McNastys who

were busy trying
to remove the
doughnuts while
simultaneously
trying to protect
their ankles,
which were
being nipped by
Dog, and their
heads, which
were being
pecked by
Pegleg Polly.
Polly was
enjoying taking
revenge for all
the times that
the McNastys
had been horrid

to her in the belly of the whale and when she had sailed with them in their ship, *The Rotten Apple*.

The children raced up the spiral staircase. They were much faster than the McNastys who never did any exercise, and who only liked long walks when the walks were being taken by people who annoyed them along a plank and into a sea of sharks.

The children and Bigwig reached the top of the staircase, sprinted into the room where Bigwig had auditioned the McNastys and ran straight into Mr Bossypants.

'Pirates!' gasped Tat. 'There are pirates in the castle.'

Mr Bossypants laughed in Tat's face, which is a very rude thing to do.

'What a silly little boy you are,' he sneered. 'Of course the castle is full of pirates, because we are making a pirate movie.'

'Please listen,' said Hetty. 'There are two real pirates here. The Ghastly McNastys, the nastiest (and I think I should add, smelliest) pirates ever to have sailed the Seven Seas.'

At that moment, the McNastys stomped into the room waving their cutlasses so wildly that they narrowly missed cutting off Mr Bossypants's head. It was a very close shave. In fact so close his moustache fell onto the floor and lay there curled up like a small dead slug.

Mr Bossypants whimpered, but he would never admit to being wrong about anything. 'You are quite mistaken. These gentlemen are not the McNastys, they are those famed thespians, the McLuvvies of the Royal Sharkspeare Company.'

'Knickers!' squawked Pegleg Polly.

The McNastys were beginning to find Mr Bossypants's self-importance very tiresome so they pushed him into a cupboard and locked the door. Then they turned to the children and Bigwig. They were between the children and the door to the room. There was no way of escape, and

Tat had used up all his ring doughnuts.

'Give us all the treasure you found.'

Hetty looked puzzled. 'We didn't find any treasure,' she said, and she showed them her empty pockets. Tat did the same, but his pockets were rather fuller, as he had an emergency ration of jam sandwiches.

The McNastys weren't interested in jam sandwiches, so Tat stuffed them back in his pocket.

The McNastys narrowed their eyes.  They were convinced the children and Bigwig were trying to trick them. Maybe they had swallowed the treasure? They waved their cutlasses dangerously and took another step towards the children.

Polly swooped down to peck their heads and got a rather fetching new feathered haircut as Captain Gruesome swung his

121

cutlass. Dog almost lost his tail to a cutlass swipe from Captain Grisly.

Tat knew that they needed to get away. He looked desperately around. He spied the big fireplace with the unlit fire laid in the grate.

'This way,' he shouted, and he ran for the fireplace, and scrambled up the chimney, followed by Hetty, who was as nimble as a mountain goat (but quite a lot prettier than most mountain goats, which often have beards. Hetty definitely didn't have a beard. Although this is what she would look like if she did).

Polly and Dog held the McNastys off as long as they could, to give Bigwig, who was slower than the children, a chance to climb up the chimney. When Bigwig and the children were out of sight, Dog took a flying leap up the chimney and landed in Tat's arms, and Polly flew up after them.

The McNastys ran to the chimney and waved their cutlasses up it, hoping to slice off a toe or two. But they had all found a nook just out of their reach.

The McNastys pushed each other to be the first to catch them, but in their struggle to scramble up the chimney, their bottoms got tightly wedged.

'Sweaty socks!' screeched Captain Gruesome.

They might still be stuck there if Captain Grisly hadn't sneezed and they shot out of the bottom of the chimney like corks out of bottles and lay sprawled in the fireplace, as if they had just been trampled by a herd of rampaging yaks trying to avoid being milked.

Captain Gruesome sat up, his head hurting. He looked in the grate where the fire was laid. He picked up a box of matches and grinned wickedly – he'd

Gruesome picked up his matches from his Seven Seas Survival Kit

smoke those hideous, horrible children out.
He struck the match and put it to the
kindling. The fire in the grate caught and
began to burn, sending a plume of smoke
upwards. Captain Grisly laughed, which
was such a horrendous sound that all the
glass in the chandelier shattered.

'Squeaky pants!' Gruesome said. 'Toasted children! What an admirably abominable idea.'

They ignored Mr Bossypants, who was banging on the door demanding to be let out of the cupboard, and peered hopefully up the chimney, waiting for the children to fall down like dead birds.

(The answer to the brainiac quiz on page 85 is number 3.)

# Chapter 9

$C$hapter 9 was so unruly I sent it to sit on the naughty step.

# Chapter 10

Polly flew up the chimney and out at the very top. Behind her she could hear Tat and Hetty scrambling upwards. She perched on a chimney pot and waited for them. From far below she could hear some voices. She put

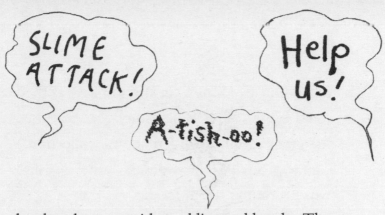

her head on one side and listened harder. The voices sounded familiar. She smiled. (Most people have no idea that birds smile, but they do.) She would have recognised both voices anywhere. One was the voice of Mrs Slime, and Mrs Slime was no friend of the Ghastly McNastys. The other was the voice of that nice but very sad woman who had fed her jam sandwiches at Little Snoring School. Polly really hadn't minded at all that the sandwiches had been very damp. The woman and Mrs Slime were in distress. (In case you were wondering, distress is not a place, but a state of mind. You never hear anyone say 'I am going to Distress' in the same way they say 'I'm just off to Bigbottoms on Sea to see the prize winning garden gnome collection.')

'Help! Help!' The women's state of mind was becoming much louder.

Polly peered down the chimney. It would be a few minutes before the children and Bigwig got to the top. She decided to investigate.

Polly did her best impression of a sparrow-hawk and dived down the walls of the castle to the very bottom. The voices were louder still and more desperate and were interspersed with sneezes.

'Help, will somebody please help us! The McNastys have locked us in here and the slime is rising.'

Polly perched on the narrow windowsill of a small barred window and peered down into the dungeon.

Mrs Slime and Miss Green were clinging to a ledge by the window, trying to escape the rising tide of slime, which was threatening to engulf them. It would not be long before they drowned in a sea of snot and tears. Mrs Slime had found a mug and

was using it
to bail out the
dungeon. But Miss
Green's distress had
created a river of tears and
Mrs Slime was sneezing so
violently it was a losing battle.
Their situation was desperate.

Polly squawked in sympathy, and seeing
Polly gave Miss Green an idea. She took a
pencil and piece of paper from her pocket

and wrote a note. She then thrust it into Polly's beak. 'Please, please take this and find Bigwig Junior the Third and give it to him.'

Miss Green had no idea if the bird understood her, but Polly's eyes gleamed brightly.

Polly spotted an old bucket lying on its side. She made a high-pitched sound like a whistle and immediately a flock of seagulls appeared.

E. Green

JUNIORS TEACHER SURVIVAL KIT

Mini Breaks

TIMES TABLES

Not headphones ear muffs

ASPIRIN

CHOCO

Teacher's Pet

Miss Green had a mug in her Junior School Teacher's Survival Kit

Polly and the seagulls had a conversation, and then Polly flew off with the note in her beak. The seagulls pushed the bucket upright and carried it in their beaks to the barred window where Mrs Slime began to fill it from her mug.

Tat hauled himself out of the top of the chimney. He had Dog under his arm and she was mewing piteously. Some of her fur was slightly singed. Hetty followed Tat. Bigwig came after, huffing and puffing. They sat down on the roof of the castle. They knew that they had had a lucky escape. Bigwig's toes were still smoking.

'Where's Polly?' asked Hetty, suddenly looking anxious.

'She's safe,' said Tat. 'She flew up the chimney ahead of me. But I don't know where she is now.'

Polly suddenly swooped down on the roof beside them. She held a slime-smeared piece of paper in her beak, which she gave to Bigwig.

My darling Bigwig,

I'm writing to say goodbye. I want to tell you that I have never stopped loving you, even though you broke off our engagement. I came to the castle with my good friend Mrs Slime hoping to see a wondrous sight and maybe catch a glimpse of you. But we encountered the Ghastly McNastys, the nastiest and smelliest pirates ever to have sailed the Seven Seas. They have thrown Mrs Slime and me into dungeon number 53, locked the door and taken away the key. We are about to be drowned by a rising tide of snot and tears. There is no hope of rescue, but if you get this note I will go to my doom knowing that you know how much I love you.

Yours, forever and for always

Emerald Green

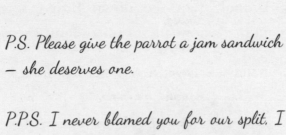

P.S. Please give the parrot a jam sandwich — she deserves one.

P.P.S. I never blamed you for our split. I always thought Mr Bossypants had something to do with it. Never trust a man with a big ego, a small heart and a false moustache.

P.P.S. Don't forget to wear your vest when the weather turns damp.

A single tear slid down Bigwig's face.
Silently, he handed Tat and Hetty the note
to read.

'So that's why poor Miss Green was so unhappy,' said Tat.

'Emerald! My love! Held hostage! By the McNastys! Here in the castle! Doomed! By my foolishness! I'll be responsible for the death of the woman I love, and her good friend Mrs Slime,' said Bigwig miserably.

'This is no time for whimpering,' said Hetty tartly. 'It's time to take action, and save Miss Green and Mrs Slime. Come on!' She hauled Bigwig to his feet.

There was a terrific flapping of wings and they were surprised to see a flock of seagulls flying towards them, taking it in turns to carry a heavy bucket which they deposited on the roof next to Tat, Hetty and Dog. It was filled to the brim with slime.

'What are we supposed to do with that?' asked Hetty, who seldom asked questions because she usually knew everything.

Tat shrugged. But from down in the depths of the chimney they heard the voices of the McNastys. He grinned. 'I know what it's for! Clever Polly!'

The McNastys had grown tired of waiting for Tat and Hetty and Bigwig to fall down the chimney. They decided that they must have got stuck like little Victorian chimney sweeps. It was very annoying. They were going to have to climb the chimney themselves.

They stamped on the fire to put it out, and then they walked into the giant fireplace and stood right underneath the chimney, looking up with their mouths wide open.

There was a sudden sloshing sound and they were deluged with slime.

# Chapter 11

The children, Bigwig and Dog climbed carefully down the side of the roof and in through an open window. Then they ran down to the audition room hoping to find the McNastys, but they had already gone.

'We must find them because they've got the key to dungeon 53 where Mrs Slime and Miss Green are imprisoned,' said Hetty.

It wasn't hard to find the McNastys. They simply had to follow the trail of dripping slime. They soon realised that it was leading to the moat – the McNastys must have gone there to wash off the worst of the slime.

On the way they ran into Mr Bossypants, whose cries had finally been heard by a passing camerawoman who had turned the key in the cupboard lock and set him free. But even though the McNastys had locked him in there, Mr Bossypants was still insistent that Bigwig and the children were mistaken to think that the McLuvvies were real pirates.

'It's their artistic temperament. They are just determined to get into character,' he said.

'Well,' said Bigwig, 'their characters are exceptionally nasty and I will not have them in my movie,' and he ordered Mr Bossypants to evacuate the castle immediately. If things turned very nasty and ghastly, he didn't want anyone getting hurt.

Mr Bossypants was very surprised. He wasn't used to being ordered about and he didn't like it. He drew himself up to his full height and puffed out his chest like a small frog. 'Smell my —' he began furiously.

'Never again,' said Bigwig firmly. 'For once you will do what you are told, and if you don't I will fire you and tell everyone that you wear a false moustache.'

The children, Pegleg Polly, Dog and Bigwig followed the trail of slime to the moat. The McNastys were there, biffing and boffing each other because they had suddenly realised that they had quite forgotten the number of the dungeon where the treasure was to be found. They broke off fighting when they saw Bigwig and the children.

'We need the key to the dungeon where you've locked Miss Green and Mrs Slime,' said Hetty urgently. 'Poor Mrs Slime can't stop sneezing, Miss Green can't stop crying and the snot levels are rising dangerously. They will drown in slime if we don't let them out.'

'You give us the treasure, and we will give you the key,' said Gruesome, and he reached in his pocket and pulled out the key and held it aloft. It gleamed tantalisingly in the sunlight.

'But we don't have any treasure,' said Tat desperately. 'We're not lying, we promise.'

The McNastys sneered. They knew that when anyone said 'I promise' they were lying because that's what they did themselves. When they were children, their mum got so tired of tripping over their broken promises that lay in bits all over their family pirate ship, that she urged them to take up pottery instead. It had been no greater a success.

'Then tell us which dungeon the treasure is hidden in,' said Captain Gruesome. Tat looked at the others.

What the McNastys dream of finding.

They all nodded, but very reluctantly.

'Tell them,' said Hetty.

'No funny business,' said Captain Gruesome with a nasty grin. 'Just to be sure you don't try to trick us, we'll take him . . .' He pointed at Bigwig. '. . . and that horrible cat called Dog and that bedraggled excuse for a parrot with us as hostages. And if we don't find the treasure when we get there, it will be the worse for them. We will cut off all Polly's feathers, slice off that cat's tail, and take Bigwig up the castle tower and throw him into the moat from a great height.'

'No —' started Hetty, but Bigwig shushed her.

'It's a deal. You hand over the key and we'll give you the number of the dungeon where the treasure can be found,' Bigwig said pleasantly, holding out his hand for the pirates to shake, which was a very brave thing to do because even though they had dipped them in the moat the McNastys' hands were still as filthy as a rubbish dump. He turned to the children. 'Hetty, Tat. Your job will be to take the key and unlock the dungeon and save my beloved Emerald and Mrs Slime.'

Tat took a deep breath and said to the McNastys, 'You'll find it in dungeon 433.'

The McNastys grinned nastily. As soon as they heard the number, they knew it was the right one.

'We'll even help you a bit more,' said Tat with a sly wink at Hetty. 'You need to look for a hidden lever which, when pulled, will reveal the hidden treasure.'

The McNastys were thrilled. They began herding Bigwig, Dog and Polly towards the castle door, all the time repeating the number out loud so they remembered it.

'Haven't you forgotten something?' said Hetty. 'The deal was that we would tell you where the treasure was and you would hand over the key.'

Captain Gruesome chuckled. 'Of course, how silly of me. I completely forgot.' He raised his arm and threw the key. It sailed over the heads of the children and for a second it seemed to hang in the air before it plunged into the middle of the moat and disappeared beneath the surface of the water.

'You should remember pirates never keep their promises,' he said wickedly, and he prodded Bigwig's bottom with his cutlass before they disappeared into the darkness of the castle.

On the way to the dungeons, the Ghastly McNastys made a detour to the room where the tank of sharks was kept. Once there, they pressed the button to release the sharks into the moat.

# Chapter 12

Tat undressed to his vest and pants. He walked towards the edge of the moat and prepared to dive in.

'You'll never find it,' said Hetty.

'It's our only chance to save Miss Green

and Mrs Slime. It may already be too late. But we can't give up hope,' said Tat firmly.

Hetty started to take off her shoes. If Tat was going into the moat to find the key, she was too, even though she wasn't nearly as good a swimmer as Tat. But Tat stopped her.

'No, Hetty,' he said. 'You must tell Mrs Slime and Miss Green that help is on its way, and tell Miss Green that Bigwig really does love her. That may stop her crying so much.'

'You are clever, Tat,' said Hetty. 'After you rescue her, Miss Green ought to give you the biggest superstar in the history of Little Snoring School.'

She ran towards the castle, but as she got there, she looked back. Tat had just dived into the water and had come up in the middle of the moat and was swimming towards the spot where the key had fallen. Hetty gasped out loud – swimming very fast towards Tat were several sharks.

'Tat!' she shouted. But Tat had already dived back under the water.

All the people who had been ushered out of the castle by Mr Bossypants had gathered on the opposite bank of the moat. They began to shout loudly. Tat surfaced, holding the key triumphantly in his raised hand. He looked at the crowd of people with astonishment. What on earth were they all pointing at?

He looked in the direction of their fingers. His eyes widened with horror, and he began swimming as fast as he could. But sharks, particularly hungry sharks, swim much faster than boys, even if those boys are champion swimmers like Tat.

The sharks were getting closer – he could feel them snapping at his heels. They had spread out in a V-formation and were

hunting him down. His breath was coming in ragged gasps, but there was no way he would be able to reach the bank and scramble out before they took a bite of his toes.

Hetty looked wildly around. She had to

help Tat. She saw his trousers on the grass, felt in the pockets and pulled out a large packet of jam sandwiches. She unwrapped it and ran along the bank towards the sharks, throwing the sandwiches into the water.

The sharks smelt them and suddenly changed direction and followed Hetty. Jam is so much tastier than boys. It is a little known fact that sharks are very fond of jam, as long as it is not apricot flavoured. Fortunately Tat's sandwiches were made with strawberry jam.

Hetty tried to eke them out as long as she could. But the sharks were hungry and had no table manners at all and they gulped the sandwiches down without even chewing them. Within seconds they had eaten all the sandwiches and were once again chasing Tat.

Hetty felt tears prick her eyes. Tat was going to be eaten!

Just then there was a commotion by the drawbridge as Mr Trout arrived and pushed his way through to the front of the crowd. Hetty gasped with excitement. She knew that Mr Trout possessed the one thing that could save Tat.

'Mr Trout,' she cried. 'Mr Trout, over here.'

But Mr Bossypants raised a hand to stop him coming further. 'No entry allowed!' he said very rudely.

Mr Trout took no notice.

'No entry,' shrieked Mr Bossypants. 'My word is law. Smell my feet!'

'No,' said Mr Trout, knocking Mr Bossypants over, 'YOU smell MY feet!' On the ground where he had fallen, Mr

Bossypants sniffed. He had never smelt anything so utterly revolting. He fainted dead away. Mr Trout ran to the middle of the drawbridge where Hetty had run to meet him.

'Quick,' said Hetty, 'take off your shoes and socks, and dangle your feet in the water.'

Mr Trout did as Hetty commanded.

Instantly the sharks lost interest in Tat.

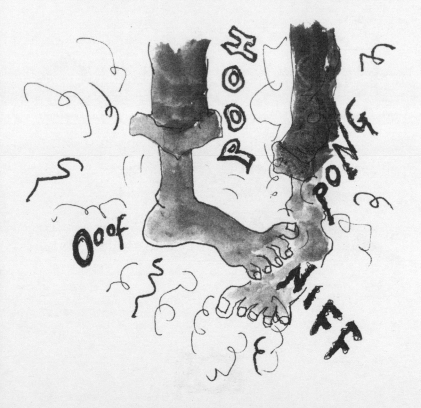

It is not well known but if there is one thing that sharks like more than jam sandwiches it is feet that smell like that kind of over-ripe Brie that is always trying to slide off the plate and make a dash for the door.

The sharks swam towards Mr Trout who removed his feet from the water just as they opened their mouths to bite off his toes.

But by then Tat had scrambled out of the moat, pulled on his clothes and, clutching the key, he and Hetty were racing towards the dungeons to unlock the door and save Miss Green and Mrs Slime.

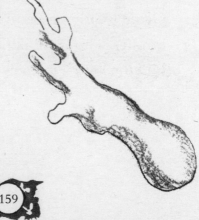

# Chapter 13

*(Lucky for everybody
except the McNastys)*

Down in dungeon 433, Captain Gruesome hunted for the treasure. Grisly was getting impatient with his brother, who was taking a very long time to find the lever. He knew that he would find it much more quickly. He was worried too that if Gruesome found the lever and got to the treasure first, he would steal it all for himself and not share any of it.

He lowered his cutlass and turned towards his brother just as Gruesome found the lever and pulled it hard. The crack in the wall began to open.

The pirates gasped. This was the moment they had dreamt of, when they would get their grubby, greedy fingers on Captain Syd's lost treasure.

In their greed they quite forgot their hostages, and Bigwig, Dog and Polly took the opportunity to tiptoe quietly away, and start running towards dungeon 53.

Meanwhile, Tat turned the key in the door

of dungeon 53, and he and Hetty stood well back as the tide of slime flowed out of the dungeon and down the corridor where it disappeared into a large drain. A second or two later, Mrs Slime and Miss Green stumbled breathlessly out of the dungeon.

'That was a close run thing. A few more minutes and Miss Green and I would have had the misfortune to have entered the record books as the first and only people to have drowned in their own snot and tears,' said Mrs Slime gratefully.

Tat and Hetty grinned, but Miss Green wasn't listening. A look of wonder and confusion on her face, she was staring down the corridor at Bigwig, who was walking towards her with his arms outstretched. He took no notice of the fact that she was covered in slime, and encircled her in his arms and laid his cheek against her cheek.

'Emerald! My love! My only love! Forgive me.'

'With all my heart,' said Miss Green and she gave him a very sticky kiss, and Bigwig didn't mind at all.

In dungeon 433, the McNastys' eyes grew rounder and rounder. The crack had opened out into a large hole. Stretched across it was the biggest, most intricate spider's web ever. The patterns on the web were exquisite. But the McNastys weren't interested in the web. Their eyes were drawn to a glistening silken silver sac right in the middle of the web.

They grinned toothlessly at each other. They had found the treasure! They wondered what was inside the silver sac. They were certain that it must be diamonds that were making it glisten so enticingly.

They looked around carefully. There was

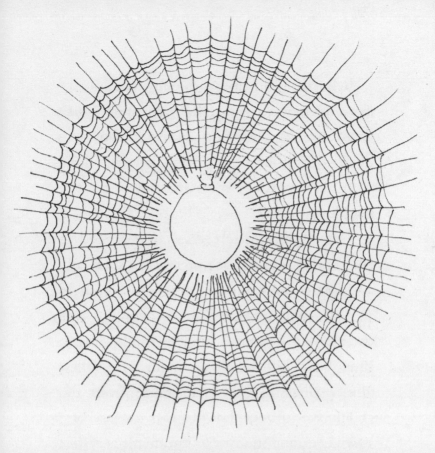

no sign of any spider. The spider must have died long ago. They stepped towards the sac. They raised their cutlasses at the same time and swiped at it.

It broke open and suddenly the floor of the dungeon was not covered with diamonds as they had expected, but was alive with thousands of baby spiders, which were swarming angrily towards the McNastys.

The McNastys screeched and turned to run, and it was at that point that they saw a sight so terrible that their legs began to wobble, their tummies did somersaults and their hearts began to beat as loudly as if a brass band had taken up residence in their chests. Bearing down on them from the ceiling was a huge, hairy spider the size of a cartwheel, and she was not at all pleased that her web and babies had been disturbed.

'Sweaty socks!' screeched Captain Gruesome.

'Squeaky pants!' whimpered Captain

Grisly, and they threw down their cutlasses and ran out of the dungeon, up the spiral staircase and out of the castle door, all the while pursued by the furious mother spider and her babies.

The McNastys ran headlong across the drawbridge. They were so scared that they completely failed to see Mrs Slime, Miss Green, Dog, Bigwig, Mr Trout, Tat, Pegleg

Polly and Hetty all standing in a line
across the middle of the drawbridge,
blocking their way.

As the McNastys got closer, the sight of them was so fearsome and stressful that Mrs Slime sneezed, creating an instant puddle of slime.

The McNastys saw the slime, but they were running at full tilt and were unable to stop in time. They slid on the slime, careered over the edge of the drawbridge and fell into the gaping mouth of a waiting shark, that swallowed them both whole.

The shark then swam all the way around the moat until it got to the side where it bordered the sea, then it leapt into the ocean and swam away.

Afterwards people said that they could just hear muffled shrieks of 'Sweaty socks!' and 'Squeaky pants!' as the shark swam towards the horizon.

Bigwig dropped a kiss on Miss Green's head. 'Nobody will be crying over the McNastys,' he said.

'No,' said Miss Green happily, 'there's no happy ever after for them, but there is for us.'

'You have these children to thank for that,' said Bigwig.

Miss Green smiled. 'I do.'

It was a few weeks later. The sun was shining, and everyone was down on Little Snoring beach where Miss Green and Bigwig Junior the Third were throwing a big party to celebrate their marriage and the end of shooting *Raiders of the Lost Shark*. Bigwig was giving up the movie business and moving to Little Snoring. He had paid Tat, Hetty, Dog and Pegleg Polly double for their roles in the movie. The Trout family budget wasn't quite so squeezed as Tat insisted he would be paying for his own new shoes out of the money he'd earned.

Mr and Mrs Trout were dancing together. Mrs Trout had decided that since Mr Trout's feet had proved so useful, she wasn't going to worry about them being smelly any more.

174

She had thrown away the leaflet advertising the special cream to cure feet that smelt like that kind of over-ripe Brie that is always trying to slide off the plate and make a dash for the door. It was just as well, as it left more room on the mantelpiece for the extra special, biggest superstar in the world, which Miss Green

had given to Tat for his bravery in helping rescue her. Hetty had got one too, but Hetty already had squillions of superstars so it meant less to her.

Bigwig tapped his glass and everyone fell silent (this did not mean they fell over but that they stopped talking) and turned to look at him.

'My friends,' he said, 'Emerald and I are both touched that you are all here to share this special day. For that we thank you. But our biggest thanks must go to Tat, Hetty, Dog and Polly who saved the day when the

day needed saving. Their bravery and quick thinking has put us in their eternal debt. So I want to give them a little present.'

He handed over a piece of parchment to Tat and Hetty. They looked at it, puzzled.

'What is this?' asked Tat.

'It's a treasure map,' said Bigwig. 'It's a map that the spider experts found when

they investigated dungeon 433 where the spider was living and where she has now happily returned with all her babies. It was hidden at the back of the space where the web was located, almost certainly placed there by the same person who designed the secret lever. So I think it is probably real. Definitely. Maybe. We could give it to the experts at the University of Greater Snoring to examine in more detail, but we thought that you and Hetty should have it first so you can try finding the

'

Hands trembling, Hetty and Tat examined the map. The writing was very faded but they could make out the few faint lines and the signature at the bottom, which said in curly letters:

*Captain Syd.*

Hetty and Tat gasped and they rushed to get their spades. They would start digging immediately while the McNastys were far, far away in the belly of the shark.

'There's no hurry, children,' said Mrs Trout. 'Those Ghastly McNastys won't be back. Nobody has ever escaped from the belly of a shark.'

'Ah,' said Hetty, 'I wouldn't be so sure. There's always a first time for everything.'

Somewhere far out at sea, the shark gave an enormous

BUUUUUUURRP...

Last ring
doughnut
for a
thousand
leagues

# THE GHASTLY MCNASTYS

## The Lost Treasure of Little Snoring

Set sail on the first Ghastly McNasty adventure!

The Ghastly McNastys are the ghastliest, nastiest pirates ever to sail the Seven Seas. But on their endless quest for treasure they come across Tat and Hetty – children who aren't going to let two thieving pirates get in their way.

The Ghastly McNastys
return in:

 # Fright in
the Night

Gruesome and Grisly
McNasty are sure they
finally know where
Captain Syd's legendary
treasure is buried. So
they scare the villagers
into thinking the place
is haunted. But
youngsters Tat and
Hetty see an
opportunity to outwit

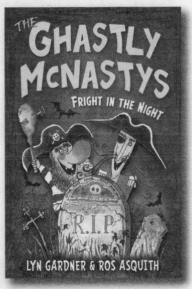

the dastardly duo by pretending to be the
ghost of Captain Syd, seeking revenge on
anyone stealing his treasure!

come aboard,
me hearties!

# ghastlymcnastys.co.uk

Go online for
pirate puzzles,
dastardly downloads,
ghastly games
and more!